A Little Princess

To Larson, my research assistant
and companion in London

ISBN 0-439-32765-2

12 11 10 9 8 7 6 5   3 4 5 6/0

Printed in the U.S.A.   14

First Scholastic printing, September 2001

Typography and cover design by Al Cetta

Title lettering by Leah Preiss

FRANCES HODGSON BURNETT'S

A Little Princess

ADAPTED AND ILLUSTRATED BY

BARBARA McCLINTOCK

SCHOLASTIC INC.
New York Toronto London Auckland Sydney
Mexico City New Delhi Hong Kong Buenos Aires

PAPA, is this the place?" whispered Sara Crewe as she clasped her father's hand tightly.

"Yes, it is, little Sara," Captain Crewe answered. "We have reached it at last."

Sara and her father were standing in front of Miss Minchin's Select Seminary for Young Girls on a London street thousands of miles away from their home in India. Sara was to attend school here for a few years. Then she would return home to her papa.

Sara's mother had died when she was a baby, and Captain Crewe was the only parent she'd ever known. They were the best of friends, and right now they were trying not to show each other how sad they were at the thought of being apart for so long.

Captain Crewe lifted the knocker on the front door and let it fall. It was opened instantly by Miss Minchin.

"What a beautiful child!" she exclaimed as she welcomed them into her school.

Sara, who did not think she was beautiful at all, guessed that Miss Minchin was just saying this to please her father. And she was right, for Miss Minchin said the very same thing to the parents of each new girl.

"Promise me you'll take great care of Sara," Captain Crewe said to Miss Minchin. "Give her anything she wants. She could never be spoiled because she is so good!"

Miss Minchin knew that Captain Crewe was rich, so she agreed.

"She's very proper on the outside, but rather unkind on the inside," Sara thought as Miss Minchin showed them upstairs to Sara's new room.

Captain Crewe decided that Sara was to have her own pony and cart, coats trimmed in fur, and dresses of silk and satin. But none of this could take away how sad Sara felt at saying good-bye. She and Captain Crewe held each other close for a long time. "I'm going to try hard to like it here," Sara finally said. She did not want her papa to worry. "I'm sure I'll learn so many new things."

"That's my girl," her father answered. "You are so brave and kind, you remind me of a little princess!"

Then Captain Crewe left. Sara watched him out the window until she could not see his carriage anymore.

The next morning Sara began classes.

When she walked into the schoolroom, the other girls began
to whisper to each other.

"She grew up in a palace in India," one girl said.

"I heard she has a pet elephant," said
another.

"Maybe she's a princess!" said a third.

Sara smiled at everyone and sat
down. She liked to learn, and she
answered every question, even
the ones that Miss Minchin
didn't know the answers to.
Miss Minchin began to
form a secret grudge
against her new pupil.

Next to Sara sat a girl named Ermengarde. Ermengarde was the slowest student in the class, and often the other girls made fun of her.

One day Ermengarde sighed. "How did you become so good at your classes, Sara?" she asked.

Sara's eyes lit up. "Schoolwork isn't so hard if you pretend. You can imagine that you're one of the people in the books you're reading, and then everything comes alive!" Then Sara added shyly, "If you like, I'll help you with your work, and then you'll see how easy it can be."

Ermengarde agreed, and from that moment on, the two girls became friends.

Although Ermengarde was her best friend, Sara was kind to everyone in class. She helped those who needed it and shared in the joy of those who did well. She quickly became the most popular girl in school.

Sara was such a good student, and so easy to like, that she soon became Miss Minchin's show pupil. When new parents came to look at the school, Miss Minchin always introduced them to Sara. Whenever the girls took walks around the square, Sara was always first in line.

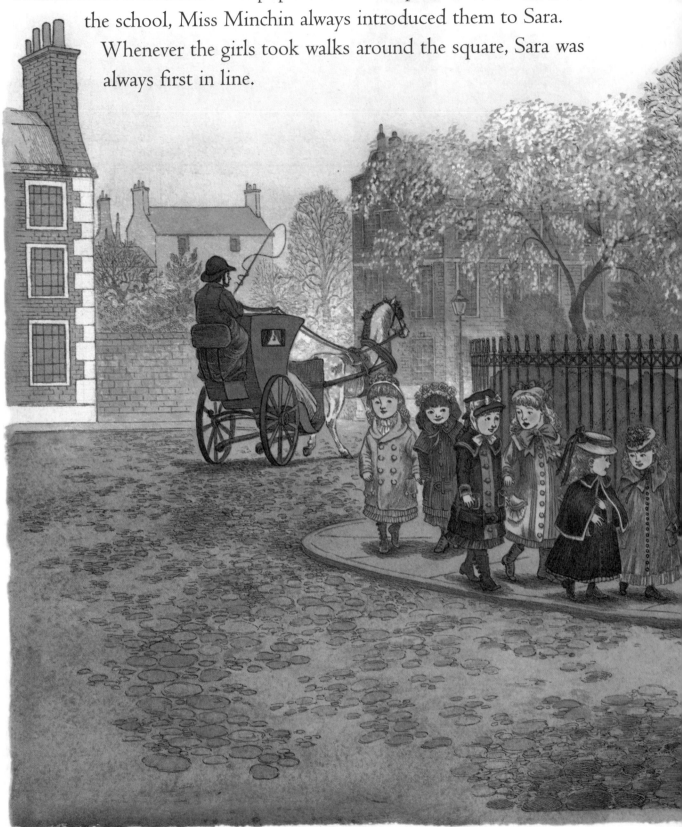

Though Sara missed her father, she tried hard to like being at the seminary, just as she had promised, and she grew to be quite happy there. She had friends, she loved her classes, and she had as many books as she wanted. And she had her father's letters, which came every day just in time for tea.

One of the things Sara loved doing best was making up stories. When Sara told her stories, they became very real to her. "They're more real than the schoolroom," she would say. Almost every afternoon the other girls would gather around her, waiting to hear what would happen next to the mermaid living in the enchanted castle, or to the prince battling the dragon. One of their favorite stories was of a princess locked in a tower by a wicked witch.

One afternoon Sara noticed Becky, the little scullery maid, listening from the top of the stairs. Sara spoke a little louder, but Becky slipped away before the story was over.

When Sara went to her room that evening, there was Becky, fast asleep in the chair.

"Poor thing," thought Sara. "She's worn out. I'll let her sleep a bit longer."

Just then a coal broke off in the fireplace, and Becky woke with a start.

"Oh, excuse me, Miss!" she cried. "I didn't mean to fall asleep! I was cleanin' the room and the fire was so warm and I was so tired and hungry, I just couldn't help sittin' down awhile."

She tried to leave, but Sara persuaded her to stay. She gave her cakes and tea and told her the rest of the story. It was the best evening Becky had ever had.

Several days later came Sara's birthday, and with it a terrible tragedy. Miss Minchin decided to give Sara a big party, with decorations and presents and a beautiful birthday cake. The whole school was invited.

Just as Sara was opening her first present, a strange man came to see Miss Minchin.

She took him into her study and closed the door. "I'm from the bank," he began, "and I've come to inform you that Sara Crewe's father has died suddenly. Before he died, he foolishly gave all his money to a friend to invest in a diamond mine. The diamond mine failed and all the money was lost. Sarah is now a pauper." The man said good day, and left.

Miss Minchin stormed into the party. She immediately sent all the girls but Sara to their rooms.

"Sara Crewe," Miss Minchin said sternly. "Your father is dead. He died without a penny. You are an orphan and have no place to go. I will allow you to stay here, but understand that you are no longer a pupil at this school. You will work for your room and board. Take off that party frock and put on your plainest black dress. Then go to the attic, where you will sleep in the room across from Becky's. You are living on my charity, and I expect you to be grateful to me. Now go."

Sara did not scream or faint. She just went very white, and without a word she did as she was told.

Once she was alone in her attic room, Sara sat quietly. Memories of her father flooded her mind. One tear came, then another, and finally Sara cried as she'd never cried before.

The next morning Sara began to work.

She swept stairs, scrubbed floors, cleaned out the kitchen stove, carried coal and water, cleaned windows, dusted furniture, hauled laundry up and down stairs, washed dishes, ran errands, and at the end of the day she taught French to the littlest students. She was always cold and hungry and tired.

Miss Minchin forbade the other girls to talk to her, especially Ermengarde. Sara's only friend was Becky, but they were both so busy that they seldom had a chance to talk. The only way Sara was able to get through the long, hard days was by pretending that she was a princess, and acting with grace and courtesy just as a princess would.

Weeks passed. Sara's clothes grew tattered and torn, and she became thin and pale.

Then the first magic thing happened.

One morning Sara found a little monkey sitting on her bed. He scampered into Sara's arms, and Sara petted his soft fur.

"You might have come right out of one of my stories!" she said softly. "But you are really real, and I believe you came through the window."

Sara looked out through the skylight. There, on the roof, was a tall Indian man.

Sara held the monkey out to him. "Is this what you're looking for?" she asked in Hindi.

The man was very surprised to be addressed in his own language. Sara explained that she had grown up in India.

"The gentleman I serve will be interested to hear about you," the man replied, taking the monkey from Sara. "He also lived in India for many years. We have just moved to London, to the house next door. Now I must go back to him. I am sorry my monkey has bothered you. He is curious and loves to explore new places."

The man bowed again and slipped through his own skylight.

After this, whenever Sara passed the house next door, it gave her great comfort to think about the people from her beloved India inside. It would have surprised her to learn that the people inside were thinking about *her*.

There came a horrible day, maybe the worst day yet.
Sara had delivered a package for Miss Minchin.
The icy rain cut through her thin dress.
She had eaten only a small crust of bread
all day, and she felt dizzy from hunger.

Suddenly, she saw a coin in the
street. She picked it up.

The smell of warm fresh bread came from a nearby bakery.
Sara went in and bought a bun, and hurried outside to eat it.

A beggar girl sat shivering on the curb. Sara realized that the girl was even hungrier and more miserable than she.

"Here," Sara said, and placed the warm bun in the girl's trembling hands.

"That girl is a little princess!" exclaimed the baker, who was watching from the window. "Practically starving, and she gave away her food. Well, if a little girl can be so generous, so can I." She opened the door and called to the beggar girl, "Come in, dear, and get warm. And there's plenty more to eat inside."

Unaware of all the good that had come from her kindness, Sara trudged home slowly. The climb up to her lonely, empty room had never seemed so long.

She opened her door. Becky and Ermengarde were there!

Ermengarde smiled shyly.

"I brought some food for you. . . . My aunt sent it to me. . . . I can't eat it all. I'm not supposed to talk to you, but . . . but . . . I don't care. I miss you!"

Sara hugged her friend. "I missed you, too!" Then, looking around the room, Sara said, "We'll pretend we have a silk tablecloth, crystal goblets, and a roaring fire. We'll have a royal banquet!" They laughed, delighted at the thought of such splendor.

All the food was soon laid out, and they were just about to eat when the door flew open.

It was Miss Minchin.

"Ermengarde!" she said furiously. "Take this food away at once! Becky—to your room! As for you, Sara, you will have nothing to eat tomorrow!"

She swept out of the room, slamming the door behind her.

Now Sara was all alone. Nothing was left of the feast.

"How stupid I was ever to pretend anything," thought Sara. "It's all just silly made-up stories. I'm not a princess—I'm a worthless drudge and I will be one forever!"

Hungry and exhausted, Sara cried herself to sleep.

But all the mermaids and princes and princesses from Sara's stories filled her dreams and comforted her while she slept.

And that night the second magic thing happened. When Sara opened her eyes, it was as if one of her stories had come to life. There was a soft, heavy blanket covering her. A fire burned brightly on the hearth, and in the middle of the room stood a table holding a silver tray of hot rolls and pastries and eggs and buttered toast and a pot of steaming hot tea.

Sara called to Becky, and together they ate a breakfast that was so delicious, they had no need to pretend it was anything else.

The next few weeks were like a wonderful dream. Each night there would be another delicious meal, and some new comfort for the room. It was magic, Sara thought, and somewhere there was a kindly magician.

Then the most wonderful magic of all happened.

One morning the little monkey popped in through Sara's window again.

"You dear little rascal!" Sara gently scolded. "Out exploring again—I'd better take you home."

Sara carried the monkey to the house next door and knocked. The Indian man appeared. He smiled and led her inside to a gentleman sitting in a chair.

"I'm Mr. Carrisford," said the gentleman. "You must be our little friend from the attic who speaks Hindi. How did you come to learn it?"

"I was born in India and lived there with my papa," Sara said. "I came here to go to school, but then my papa died, and I have been working ever since."

"And what was your papa's name?" the man asked gently.

"Captain Ralph Crewe," she said. "I'm Sara Crewe."

"Great heavens!" Mr. Carrisford shouted, leaping out of his chair. "I've found you!"

Sara stepped back, confused.

Mr. Carrisford caught his breath. "I was your father's friend. He gave me all his money to invest in a diamond mine. We had just gotten news that the mine was worthless when he died. A few weeks later we discovered diamonds, more than have ever been found anywhere. I've been looking for you to take care of you as your dear papa would have. I only knew that you were in a boarding school, but I didn't know where. And here you were, just next door!"

Trembling, Sara sat down. Mr. Carrisford told her that he and Ram Dass, the Indian man, were the magicians who had transformed her room, for the sake of Sara Crewe, the little lost orphan girl. "In our wildest imaginings we never once guessed that the attic girl and Sara Crewe were one and the same."

Laughing and crying, Sara thanked them over and over again for helping her. Mr. Carrisford just held out his arms, and without another word, Sara ran into them.

Sara never returned to Miss Minchin's seminary. Instead, she stayed with Mr. Carrisford, and Becky came to live with them too. And Ermengarde came over every Sunday for tea.

Sara now had everything that any little girl could want.
But she never forgot her terrible days in the attic. For the
rest of her life Sara was kind and good to everyone she met.
She shared her wealth and her loving heart with those in
need, and especially with children, just like a true princess.